Notes of a
SANE
WOMAN

Notes of a SANE WOMAN

scenes from a life that dares to be lived

Patricia L. Goss

Conari Press
Berkeley, California

Printed in the United States of America
Cover: Patricia L. Goss design
Photo by Warren Samuel

ISBN: 0-943233-42-9

This book is dedicated to a few women in my life:
Mammy Dawgs, Hymer, Dooh-Dah & Kimberly,
Gram Ruth, Anty, cuz Leese & 'Cole, Soozie,
Dog Lips, Lynn, Ruebin, Ain't Vic -n- Beta,
Airport Neeta, Za and mamma Za, Booby,
Kimbo, Dianne with 2 n's, Cammielle,
The Lib-ness, Gurdjieff's mother, Claudia Jai,
EJay, La-u-ren, Pooch, Charlene, B. Diehl,
Debbie Tilt, Selena in Taos, and the white blue
sparkling depths of love in my Geemaw's eyes.
Those same eyes that love me and hold me.
It was through those eyes that I learned
how to save my life . . .

with love and a little bit of humor . . . .

Forewording Intrologue

You want to know about this "sane woman," Patricia? My pleasure . . . I know more than anyone else about her. I'm her sister. We were mistaken for twins for the first half of our lives and that's where I get the authority to let you know right here in the beginning of this book that she is a statistical oddity. Why? Because anyone coming from such a messy childhood shouldn't have turned out so well.

Dysfunctional was too good a word for our family. Have you ever had to fill out one of those questionnaires where you grade the quality of your home life by checking the appropriate box marked yes or no and if you checked all the yes boxes, it meant that you should "call this number immediately"? Well, we could have checked all those boxes–if they had written the questionnaire in "Toddler" (the only language we could understand at the time). We didn't know that the abuse was wrong. For a long time it just seemed that it was the way life was supposed to be, that is until the stripes on our legs didn't match the stripes on our dresses. It wasn't pretty. I'll spare you the gory details. In spite of it all we grew up to love our parents and, as the wounds heal, we've also learned to love someone even more important. We learned to love ourselves.

The surprise. Patricia. She is my hero (soon to be yours). She is here and accountable for being here. She not only looks at you, she sees you. She not only listens to you, she feels you. When she puts her pen to paper, it has the perfect blend of humor, intellect and truth. I say perfect blend, because as you read and re-read these pages, you will find truths you missed the first time, funnies that weren't so funny before, and a perspective that will add mud to your water or vice versa.

Sometimes people who paint the truth are alarming. Patricia is alarming. She not only seeks out the alarm clocks in life, but she creates the alarm and then takes

responsibility for her creation. She has enough ambition for many, and it seems to be geared almost entirely toward self-discovery.

As her closest confidant, I've witnessed her take on her resistance to life as an opportunity to wake up and reformulate herself. Using the junk from her life as reminders to engage with what is in front of her so as not to end up catnapping her life away. This girl is learning how to smell the coffee in a big way.

I'm no critic of literary works, but she has captured a lot of presence here. You will enjoy her humor and her seriousness. Thought provoking. Original. Something for everyone, whether he or she likes it or not.

HOLLY RILEY

Hymer

MARRIANNE K. McDONNELL

I've been doing therapy for a few months, and with a lot of hard work we've discovered that my heart was broken when I was about two and never set quite right.

We uncovered some horrid abuses that had long been swept under the rug and forgotten. Returning as an adult to the experiences of my youth hurt more than anything I've ever known. I didn't realize I had so much pain. You could say we had to go back in and break my heart again . . .

in order for it to heal correctly.

NOTE NUMBER

2

I used to agonize over not knowing which fork to pick up at the dinner table. Constantly looking for a nod from the grown-ups that I had made the right choice. What I would put myself through for a moment of recognition! It seemed as though my desire to do what was right in the eyes of the adults would lead me forever through a life of suffering and pain–that I must undergo endless hardship and unworthiness to receive their approval.

The future looked bleak.

Then one day I realized that they didn't know which fork to pick up either. I grew up right there, a little. I was glad for my discovery and a little dismayed, too. A loss and a gain. Letting go of them for direction made me sad, but I felt good about my own ability to make a choice.

Suddenly the whole thing felt quite comical. But I still had to check the room to make sure I was the only one there before I started laughing.

WARREN SAMUEL

HOLLY RILEY

I went to the edge of reality and stood there in the dark: looking out with my toes hanging over like the swimmer at her mark, waiting for the gun to go off. To jump out into the abyss. To fly.

If I'm so brave then why am I trembling?

I can't hide forever. Sooner or later I'm going to have to jump off this edge. Maybe I'll find out who I truly am.

Slivers of light dance in the darkness, mocking me. Maybe if I stand a little farther out on the edge . . . reach a little further . . . look a little harder, I'll see a net.

Maybe not.

Eventually, through persistence and determination, I will succeed in creating a way of thinking for myself that works in this world.

Either that or finish off the rest of that hard salami in the fridge.

Nothing gets done when two people are talking at once. Especially when both of them are me.

When the chatter gets too loud, the only thing for me to do is walk away, read a book, take a nap, or possibly return to the refrigerator to contemplate that hard salami some more.

The possibilities are limitless.

My head is empty unless *I* put something in there.

WARREN SAMUEL

Yeah. All this running naked in the wind. Discovering my denial and pain.

All the hurt.

All the loneliness.

After all this therapy, I know now what really happened (growing up with abuse as one of the four basic food groups). The cat's outta the bag. And it hurts more than any striped and bloody back.

I abandoned myself right out of the gate. I took on the unworthiness I judged that my parents held for me. So I tried to do everything I could to get as far away from me as possible. And it worked.

Up til now.

NOTE
NUMBER

I hate this red fingernail polish. (Or am I resisting
my real feelings about red fingernail polish?)
Maybe if I explored my feelings about red fingernail
polish, I might find that I can wear all colors.

Maybe I'd find the rainbow that I am,
and wouldn't that be frightening?

WARREN SAMUEL

It might be emotionally profitable to take an objective look at how I deprive myself of the simple pleasure of being. Because of my conditioning to live in the future or the past, I neglect the moment I'm in. I turn the present into a nostalgic semivoid and I miss the moment. That big plate of pancakes with syrup in front of my face suddenly tastes like a big stack of cardboard.

A good ten years can go by if one isn't paying attention.

I watched an authority on TV talking about over-
breeding dogs. He found that certain breeds aren't
caring for their young anymore because of the strain
on their gene pool. (Why would a pug-nosed dog
want to raise and care for four or five pups that can
hardly breathe?)

Is this in any way a reflection of our human spirit
denying itself? That if we continue to focus on
outward appearances instead of inner understanding,
we may have that same fragmentation show up in
our children, thereby making them undesirable also,
simply because they mirror the inadequacies of their
own parents?

No wonder I got beat up when I was a kid. I remind-
ed my parents of themselves.

Donald McIlraith

NOTE NUMBER

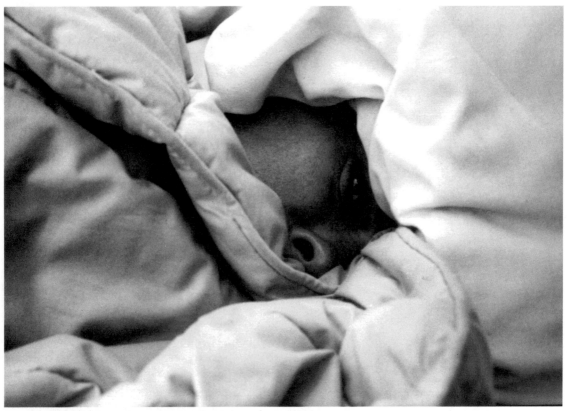

I want to give up. I just don't have enough energy to fight anymore. I don't even have enough energy to imagine what would happen if I never got out of bed again. This game of fighting over right or wrong, too hot or too cold, too blue or too red has taken all the air out of me. I don't have enough energy to form an opinion about it all. I'm sick of opinions. Even my own opinions are boring.

I'm more concerned with how to put my pillow over my head
so I can shut out all impressions and still be able to breathe.

I consider being able to rise to the occasion and reach beyond my fears of rejection to be a significant gain in my personal growth. It's the only way I've found to be absolutely sure that my dread was a dream meant to keep me forever sleeping.

The world is so much more fun when I'm wide awake.

CHRIS BLISS

You know that anxious feeling? The one where you don't know whether to freeze or run? Like standing in line at the fair to get on the "Zipper" for the first time (not knowing that after the ride is over, your face will hurt from laughing so hard that it'll be stuck in the smile position).

My friend is resigning from her job today. She outgrew her position of looking up at the mountain to wanting to see over and beyond the mountain. She got tired of being pushed around for the last thirty or so years. Tired of the "yes sir" and "no sir." Tired of having all her decisions snipped just after they began to bud. Tired of those in higher positions taking credit for the sweat of her own brow and, finally, she got very tired of the weaklings below her who used everything in their power to bring her down so they could do a two-step on her heart.

She's also standing in line to get on the Zipper. I wonder if she knows that her face is going to get stuck in the smile position, too . . . .

NOTE
NUMBER
12

Everything is locked up tight.

Nothing can get in.

Nothing can get out, either.

CHRIS BLISS

Last night we ordered take-out Chinese.

Pulling out the slip of paper, I saw
"Depart not from the path which fate
has you assigned."

Immediately I picked up another cookie.

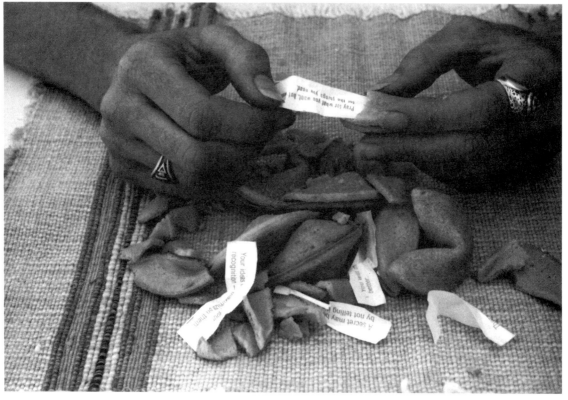

WARREN SAMUEL

Are we all alchemists?

I sit back and watch society take raw substance and transform it
into something else. We can take a tiny spark of energy and the
next thing you know we're on the phone to Italy talking to our
Great Aunt Lydia. We're very good at turning dirt into concrete
and sand into glass, teaching dolphins to jump through rings of
fire, crossbreeding roses, and concocting chemicals in the form
of tiny little pills to take the edge off our day.

I wonder what would happen if we took this magic
of transformation and used it internally . . .

like on, say, a bad habit or a negative attitude?

CHRIS BLISS

N O T E
NUMBER
15

High school brought many surprises . . . two of them being
pubic hair and the desperate need to be needed. Then there
was peer pressure, the dread of rejection, seeking immediate
gratification while in a constant state of fear. I couldn't help
being scared that there could be someone out there who
might want to know me more than I wanted to know myself.

Or that there might *not* be.

WARREN SAMUEL

I've always hated peas and lima beans. But as a kid, when I would go over to Geemaw's house and she'd serve one or the other, I'd taste them even though I didn't like them.

I thought there might be the slightest possibility that I could have changed my mind when I wasn't looking.

When I'm in pain, it seems to last forever. A lonely darkness. But as time passes, a ray of hope opens up inside of me and I can sense unlimited possibility just around the corner.

Is this the proverbial light at the end of the tunnel?

Do I have to walk through that long, lonely tunnel of darkness before I can bathe in that shaft of light way down yonder?

I guess I do . . .

Either that or sit here in the muck and mire, picking dirt out from underneath my fingernails and hope some brave knight (wearing a fine Italian suit and one of those swank silk ties) will come along to offer me the Grail full of eternal life and slake this insatiable thirst.

If those are my choices, I'd better start walking.

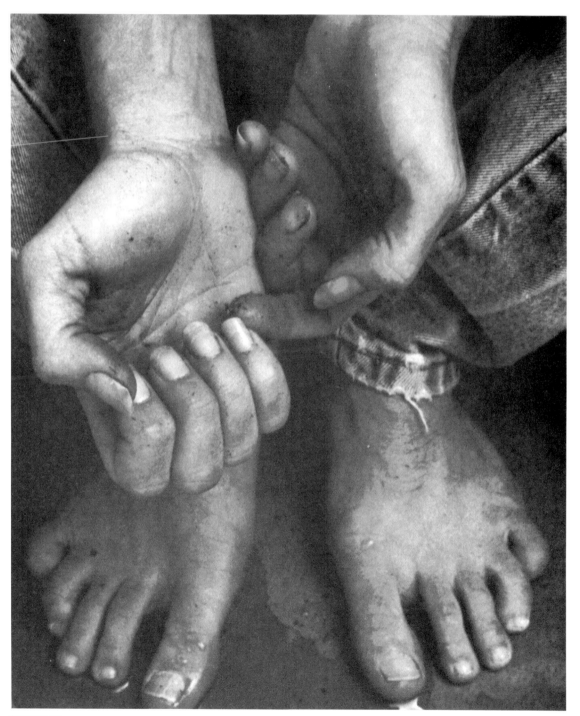

NOTE
NUMBER
18

I got my first zit when I was eighteen. Breasts showed up
a little later. The sex stuff wasn't far behind with intense
hormonal discoveries.

Does this mean I was a late bloomer?

It all came and went so fast.

It seems like everyone I ever loved has left me, or I abandoned them before the possibility arose that I might get hurt by their leaving.

And now I sit here in the midst of all this pain and loneliness, considering the thought of abandoning myself too.

CHRIS BLISS

There's a saboteur living in my midst. An enemy agent. A deliberate
subversive. She perverts and corrupts me by undermining my faith.

She's a brat. A puny thing with big black circles under her eyes from
all those sleepless nights of plotting and planning ways to rob me of
being whole. I've tried to kill her, but she won't die.

How can I love one such as this? Could I have missed something?
If everything I perceive is in some way a reflection of myself, then
she is me. And if she is me then I can love her, can't I?

If she's so good at vandalizing my efforts to be whole, consider the
empowering effect she'd have on my life if she felt safe in my home.
Or, possibly, in my heart.

I think I'll invite her in.

MARRIANNE K. McDONNELL

What happened to those childlike qualities of risk-taking that just came with the job of being alive? Have I gotten so comfortable and safe in my behavior that I'm unwilling to experience the new? Could there be more to me than I see? If so, where do I find it?

In a book?

A therapist?

A guru?

Possibly scrawled on the bathroom wall?

I think the answer lies in risking. I'm not talking about jumping out of airplanes or scaling mountains, although that may be close.

I'm talking about something more difficult–like somersaulting half the length of the local mall, or inviting the most intimidating person I know out to lunch and telling him how I feel . . . or exploring something in my own heart that I'd packaged up very neatly and tucked away for dead.

WARREN SAMUEL

I've always considered myself to be quite an "edge-walker." Now that this risking business is in the forefront of my thinking, I see I've been just an adrenaline junkie.

Hanging around in vulnerability is the place to be–and I never have to leave my chair to go there. I simply remember that I don't know anything . . . and it's the same for everyone else.

If Prince Charming came and knocked on my door, offering
me gifts of love, passion, and safety as he swept me off my feet,
kissing me hard, long, and good . . .

I'd never know it.

I'd be so busy processing my feelings that the chance to really
experience the moment would have slipped through my heart
like hot water through a spaghetti strainer.

I think I'm on the brink of mass inner mayhem. Either that or it's time to go home and take off all restrictive clothing. There's a hollow pit inside of me that begins in the space between my eyes. Every time I open my mouth to speak small animal-like guttural sounds spew forth. This pit is a muddy trap for all those animals. It's raining and every time they try to escape, their muddy paws meet a landslide of wet, brown slime that drags them back. No escape, just the timeless dripping of the rain into doom. A dark and muddy doom. A wet, dark, and muddy doom. A wet, dark, damp, and muddy doom . . . No, wait–a slimy, wet, dark, damp, and muddy doom. No! No, wait–a seeping dankness that holds a slimy, wet, dark, damp, and muddy doom . . . Wait! I got it! A slithering, seeping dankness that holds a slimy, wet, dark, damp, and muddy doom. Here it is! This is it! A creeping fog with a seeping dankness that holds a slimy, wet, dark, damp, and muddy doom.

Yeah. That's it.

Patricia L. Goss

(I've discovered that, after taking the time to wallow
around in my misery, like a dog in dead squirrel guts,
I feel much better.)

N O T E
NUMBER
24

I mustn't allow myself to look over my shoulder.
My visions and goals are so high that if I look back,
I may realize how far I have to fall and give up
the entire idea altogether.

WARREN SAMUEL

You approach me with wild abandon and only request my spare change. Your look is bland, without depth of intention. Do you think the reason why people avoid your eyes and automatically hand it over is because they're afraid to see their own despair? A glimpse of their own life? Perhaps witness the universes they're missing?

If I give you my spare change, where will you go? Is this the only link between you and me? Why do I care?

What will you do with all those quarters?

NOTE
NUMBER
26

I need a large rasp. I want to grind off all the rough edges
of my judgments and soften them into opinions.

That way it would be easier to walk through the doorways
of experience without any predetermined ideas as to the
outcome. Maybe I'd perceive each moment as it truly is.
Possibly learn something new.

And wouldn't that be refreshing?

Thirteen years is a long time to hang on to a friend who's convinced that the monkey-see-monkey-do theory is the safest way to go through life.

Another lemming that is sure that swimming is only meant for the fishes.

After all that time I knew that if he had to count on hope from others instead of himself he was, indeed, hopeless. And my life is better spent in company with people who are willing to test the waters and learn a few strokes on their own.

DONALD MCILRAITH

LIBBY J. NICHOLSON

The long disappointment I've had for my father's inability
to show me unconditional love has ended.

I've come to terms with not having the power to control
or repair a love that was never enough for me.

He failed to meet my expectations and hopes.

He missed the mark on how I believed one should act if
one loved another.

I just couldn't forgive him

. . . until I forgave myself for wanting him to be someone he wasn't.

It's like having a bad attitude toward a pine tree for not being an
oak. The tree couldn't care less how I feel and, will continue to be
exactly what it is. A pine tree.

NOTE
NUMBER
29

I asked Libby why she didn't answer her phone today.

She said she spent the whole afternoon reading an
instruction book on how to love herself. She got
stuck on the chapter that teaches you how to give
yourself a hug. Apparently her hands were full
when I called.

Nothing is impossible. No limits. No boundaries, fences, or gates. Wide-open freedom, beauty, and only ten more car payments left.

Now *that* is pure unadulterated joy.

LISA M. GORMAN

There was a time in my life when I looked across the room and saw someone I wanted to sail away with. . . .

It didn't take me too long to pack up my belongings and abandon my own ship.

Twelve years passed before I realized that I had lost myself.

These days I spend my time looking for sunken treasure . . . and the gems I've uncovered are priceless. One of them is the yearning to recover. I found this jewel buried so deep inside myself that I'd almost lost hope of ever being the captain of my own ship. But just when I was about to forsake myself yet again, I realized that *I* had handed myself over in the first place. If I can give everything over to someone else, then I also have the power to reclaim myself as my own.

Now it's just me and the wide open sea.

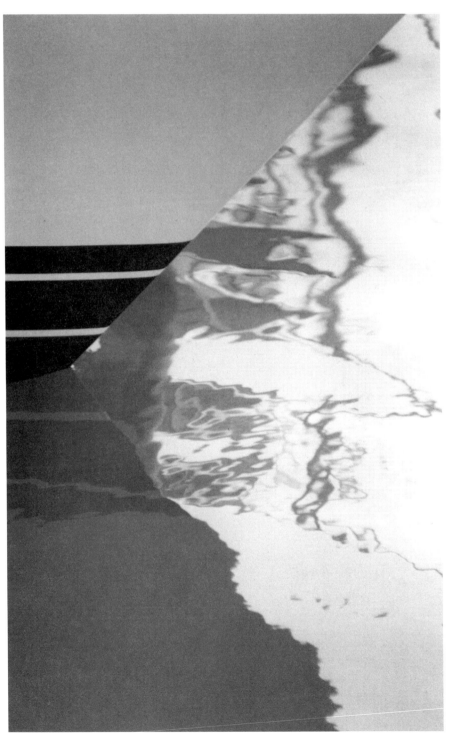

NOTE
NUMBER
31

PATRICIA L. GOSS

I don't know what to do. When I was young my father used to say
"when you don't know what to do, do nothing."

That doesn't make sense anymore. It doesn't work. The only thing it
ever got me was more "nothing." I want to do *something*, now. I *can*
do something, now. I'll just have to make it happen. Figure it out.
Create it. Do it. Believe it. Be it.

If I want to, say, do the Twist, the only way to find out is to get up
right now, this minute, and do a quick jig.

Instead of sitting on my butt and imagining winning first prize in that
great big sock-hop in the sky, I've got to get up right now, this minute,
before the music stops. I don't want the answers after I'm dead.
I want them now while I'm alive and still able to dance.

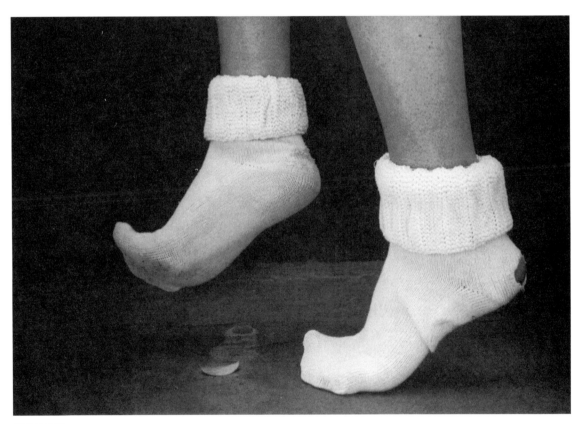

Warren Samuel

N O T E
NUMBER
33

For so long it seemed that all I heard was the constant chatter of voices in my head. Like a family of monkeys in a tree fighting to speak. Fighting for the spotlight. Then one day I kicked them all out. I sent them home and put a sign on the door of my mind that read

NO BLABBERS!

Now everything is quiet. No noise or chatter except for this little voice pleading for the silence to always stay . . .

and even that voice is getting smaller.

Presence evokes presence. Being evokes being. Sincerity evokes sincerity.
Patience evokes patience.

I guess it's safe to say that if you ever wanted to check up on yourself and
see where you're at . . . just look around at your environment and how you
feel about it. Everything you see will be you.

WARREN SAMUEL

LISA M. GORMAN

The big blame game. We point fingers at each other. We try to see who can talk louder. We compete for the "important moment." We cover up our fear and shine the light on the other person to avoid being caught. We sharpen our tools of subterfuge and artifice instead of honesty and openness. We present sham as true accountability without even blinking.

Instead of really sharing ourselves, all that we do is trade off who gets to be right.

When is everyone going to be ready to live differently? When are we going to dicover the excitement self-honesty can bring? Has courage become another grocery store item on the bottom shelf behind the stewed tomatoes?

I just realized I'm swimming by myself. I hate it. I thought I was working on a team with a common cause. You know. One for all and all for one. I know now it's not that way. There's always going to be someone hanging around the deep end who's hoping to keep me from that next breath of air.

Now I'm on the mark alone and I haven't got a choice but to reach for the other edge of the pool. All of my fellow swimmers are looking at the clock

. . . and the gun went off a long time ago.

HOLLY RILEY

NOTE
NUMBER
37

Lynn told me today that she hasn't had sex in so long

. . . she thinks she got her virginity back.

Maybe I'll surpass even my own limits, and God will reveal Himself to me.
Or is this kind of experience limited to saints and martyrs . . . and the
beggar who sleeps on the bench?

MARIANNE K. MCDONNELL

NOTE
NUMBER
39

I'm going to love myself with all my might. I'm going to go beyond my wildest imagination (which is pretty much on the extra-large size as it is).

I get to blow my own skirt up! I get to quit denying my passion for being alive. I get to BE!

I just gave myself a hall pass.

The little girl in me mindlessly swings on the "cattle ropes" while waiting in line at the bank. And twirls full circle on the back of her heel, so perfectly, in the middle of the marble lobby floor. She likes the way elevators make her tummy swirl. She sits patiently on my knee and waits quietly for me to finish with my seriousness.

Her courage honors me.

When I grow up—I want to be just like her.

WARREN SAMUEL

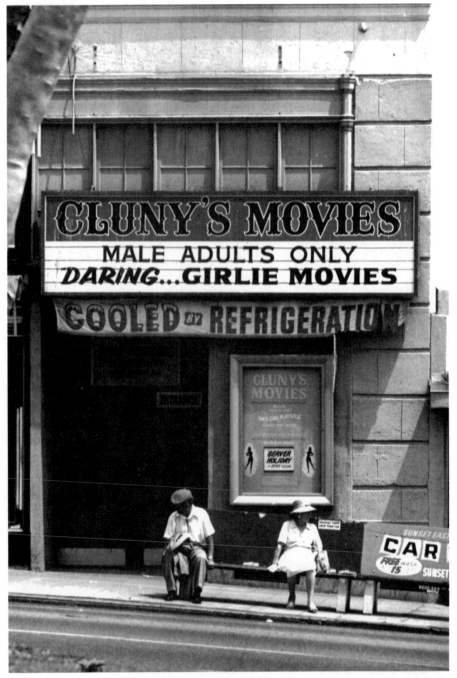

WARREN SAMUEL

I've discovered that my satisfaction doesn't come from what other people think is good or bad . . . anymore. If someone doesn't like what I do or say, it's okay. If it's not okay with me, then I'm the one with the problem, because I'm the one with the opinion.

Of course this bluebird of understanding didn't just fly in the window one day singing sweet chords of truth in my ear.

It's more like a piece of hard candy that got stuck in my throat and hurt like hell for a while. Until I could gather up enough saliva in my mouth to wash it down.

. . . Or a long time runnin' against a hard wind, with a sour outlook and a shrunken heart.

NOTE
NUMBER
42

We meet and my first response is to hug you tight.
But I don't. I'm just like everybody else.

Ultimately I resist myself.

We're all walking around with invisible straightjackets
on. Still, we manage to shake hands and act as though
nothing were out of place.

It's as if we limit our experiences according to our
judgments. We respond to the moment with an idea
from the past. We continue to go through life with
blinders on and a feed bag wrapped around our heads.

Where did denial of our true selves come from?
Is it something that's handed down from generation
to generation? What would happen if we changed
the rules and everyone started hugging without first
checking the image they have of themselves?

I think I'm going to start hugging without a cue.

PATRICIA L. GOSS

I looked at you tonight for a very long moment, Mom, and I saw how beautiful you are. I watched you talk and laugh, having a grand old time. Everyone loves you.

We held each other to say good-night and we both felt so good that we started crying–and I'm only staying two doors down.

It was almost like the first day of school. I cried then, too. Was that day as hard for you as it was for me even though I knew that the school playground butted up against our backyard?

I don't think that words could ever put right the way you fill my heart, Mom. I know now . . . you're just as close as my heart is to me. I don't have to touch it to feel it beating inside.

N O T E
NUMBER
44

Debbie met a nice guy and said yes when he asked her to marry him. They went all the way . . . you know, got the blood tests, moved in together, talked and dreamed of a bigger apartment.

Then a couple of weeks ago she found out that Joe was a closet junkie who lied to her about his blood test. Today she tested positive for the HIV virus.

My first reaction was to kill Joe, until I realized that he already had plastic tubes sticking out of every hole in his body. His dirty little needle, laced with his own denials and lies, has altered the lives of everyone around him.

And then there's Debbie. Her courage and love is enough to make me turn around and look at myself and see that I have denial, too. I'm just not using a needle to hide from it.

WARREN SAMUEL

I remember one day when I was little my sister Holly and I were riding in the backseat of the car. Mom was driving, and I asked Holly what color the leaves of a passing tree were.

She said: "Green, stupid."

I said: "How do you know?"

She said: "Everybody knows that leaves are green."

I said: "How do you know that what you call green doesn't look blue to me and that we both just call it green so we can talk about it, but what we each *really see* are different colors?"

She said: "Mom! Tell Patty to stop it!"

I was driving home from work one day singing at the top of my lungs to a tune on the radio when two handsome men in a red convertible pulled out next to me.

I immediately stopped singing. As soon as there was a safe distance between our cars I tried to pick up the lyrics again, but couldn't.

I had made myself sick. In a matter of seconds I had hidden my true self in order to maintain my preconceived image. I realized I wanted to be noticed by those two young bucks in a certain way. Not for who I truly am.

You could say I was driving the car from the seat of my pants.

Every man, woman, tree, or pebble has a purpose. Made or man-made. So what is the function of a relationship? It's one of those questions whose tonal qualities ring on . . . long after the tolling of the bells.

To first experience a relationship to its fullest potential shouldn't the intentions of each party be defined and then expressed?

Undefined intent in a relationship is like spitting in the wind. You can aim wherever you like–you just don't know where it's going to land. I guess if I didn't care about the outcome, spitting would be a good thing.

Marianne K. McDonnell

Things that are meaningful to me may not necessarily be meaningful to someone else. My banana cream pie may be someone else's liver and onions.

Could this mean that the people who are going to hell may not necessarily feel bad there? That hell may be the perfect place for murderers and the subjugators of the weak to see their own true selves and possibly evolve?

Taken in this context, hell could be a good thing for everyone.

Marianne K. McDonnell

NOTE
NUMBER
49

I've got it! I already am what I'm struggling to reach.
I just have to figure out which knob is the volume
and which one's the channel changer.

What if the two thieves who were nailed to the cross and died with Jesus are similar to the two thieves who live in my heart? One says yes and the other says no. One says "good girl" and the other says "bad girl." Could Christ be the one who's right in the center without judgment? Could recognizing this bring understanding? Balance? Love? Is that why he was in the middle?

I have the will to choose. I can listen to the thieves and act on their words, or I can be still and experience the balance.

LIBBY NICHOLSON

Isn't it amusing sitting in the afterglow of a grand fear only to realize
that you're the one who created it in the first place? Isn't it great to be
able to turn around and look at yourself after you've beaten yourself up
for some wrongdoing or another and have a knee-slappin' guffaw and
cry aloud to no one in particular?

Who made up
these rules in
the first place
and why am I
following them
without taking
a closer look
at the author?!

WARREN SAMUEL

NOTE
NUMBER
52

A great teacher once said, "You can never be too close to the ones you love."

I've found that even picking a large piece of hairy lint
off someone's coat sleeve can take a great deal of courage.

We've all been conditioned to think that to get something we want takes a lot of time, arduous work, sweat, tears, pain, and many failures before we get it, and then we may be too old to enjoy it, play with it, ponder it, or be it . . .

The little voice that lives inside my heart tells me that's a lie.

I know now that believing in all that noise is what's kept my spirit down in the first place. I had to discover for myself that I am capable of changing things. I'm capable of moving mountains, 'cause I'm the one who put the mountain there in the first place.

LISA M. GORMAN

I'm thirty-four years old and I just realized why I don't like snapdragons.

When I was really little, my Uncle Rod picked one and showed me how a snapdragon snaps. It scared the hell out of me and I've given them a wide berth ever since. I can recall walking in the gutter instead of the sidewalk if snapdragons were guarding the green of someone's lawn or gate. Until just a few weeks ago.

Rae and I were laying down new shelf liner and decided to take a lunch break and walk downtown. Lo and behold there were snapdragons gracing a garden along our way, and she plucked one and made it snap (I was brave and followed suit).

Except there was a big difference.

My snapdragon was menacing and mean with a wide gaping jaw that could take a large chunk out of a small child's leg and swallow it whole.

Rae's snapdragon smiled and talked with a French accent.

I realized then and there that Uncle Rod had introduced me to snapdragons upside down. I also realized that it was likely there were other things introduced to me upside down. Like white bread will kill you, and if you cross your eyes for too long they'll get stuck like that. Or how about if you ignore it, it will go away?

RIGHT WAY

WRONG WAY

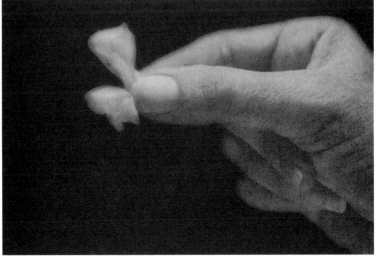

Is denial of our true selves a game we create to keep us from being who we really are?

Why would we invent something like that?

If we claimed authorship of our denial wouldn't it bring more clarity of purpose?
Could denial be good like castor oil?

What gift does denial have for us then? (I have quite a list so I'd like to know.)

Maybe it comes in a coupon book like the old S&H Green Stamps, and we just
take our collection to the redemption center and hand it in for our gift of choice.

I wonder if I have enough stamps yet to get the gift I want? And I'm not talking
about that black strapless number or those skyscraping leather pumps, either.
I'm talking about one of the big one's.

Like patience, maybe.

WARREN SAMUEL

NOTE
NUMBER
56

Sometimes it's difficult to balance my vulnerability with my strength. My femininity is mistaken for weakness, and those who would devour a tender thing begin to gather around. They get just a tad too close, sensing an easy mark. They don't realize that underneath this lacy glove I wear is a fist of iron.

CHRIS BLISS

If I could move forward and backward at the same time, I'd be there by now.

I figured it out.

I don't hate Dad anymore.

First of all, I gave myself permission to feel how I really felt about him, and the truth was

1) I didn't like anything about him
2) I didn't have to like anything about him

After that I found a small soft space that was labeled "Dad." And I saw that I love that space just because he is "Dad."

Very simple.

I got bored with punishing him for just being himself.

PATRICIA L. GOSS

NOTE
NUMBER
59

I used to hear trumpets in the space before waking yet not quite dreaming . . .
or that space before dreaming yet not quite awake. The sound was so pristine.
It was as if I were the sound itself. Changing constantly. Each note new and
then gone. Those were profound moments even though I didn't know exactly
what it all meant. They widened my vision even though my eyes were closed.

I laugh now because that's how we all are. Constantly changing. Each chord
to be struck in the next moment is entirely different than the one before it.
Never to be repeated.

Trying to hang on to and define them only sours the sound.

I've decided to indulge my impulses more often. Jump for no reason. Talk to a spider instead of mercilessly destroying it. Give James the panhandler and his dog some canned goods instead of the usual fifty cents. Honk my horn at the four-way stop sign on the way to the market because nobody can decide whose turn it is. Send my mother flowers on *my* birthday. It seems to relieve a little of that imaginary yet colorful brain hemorrhage I've been nursing for the last twenty years.

LISA M. GORMAN

Acceptance—what is it? Is it when I quit fighting and resisting things for the way they are?

Is it the state of being without judgment or opinion?

If I learned acceptance, would that mean I could fully experience the snap-crackle-pop of the moment?

Just imagine what that would mean:

1) No more prejudice.
2) No more sham.
3) No more duplicity.
4) No more bad attitudes on the freeway.

Kinda makes you dizzy just thinking about it.

Marianne K. McDonnell

NOTE
NUMBER
62

Does anybody really put as much toothpaste on their toothbrush as in the commercials?
Does this in any way reflect the state of our thinking, or should I just change the channel
and find something to look at that doesn't bother my mind?

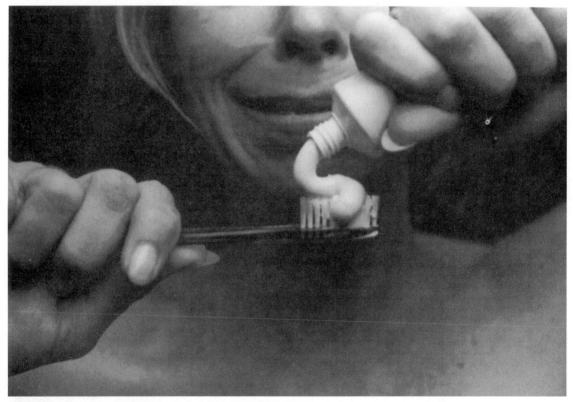

WARREN SAMUEL

I keep two clean wine glasses in my dish drainer.

Just in case . . .

perhaps . . .

maybe someone will drop by and think I had previous company.

NOTE
NUMBER
64

PAUL HUGHES

Is the "little self" the one who likes chocolate

instead of vanilla?

And the "God self" the one who likes both?

Now that I have some distance between myself and my pain, I can see *me* in the full light of being.

I don't have a shadow anymore . . . the light seems to hit me from all sides.

LIBBY NICHOLSON

I want to pass through that great divide.

The one between hope and fear. Haves and have-nots. Prey and hunter.
You know .... duality. Feeling as though I deserve something but then,
when I'm truly honest with myself, knowing that what I really feel is that
I don't deserve it–or it wouldn't be so difficult to achieve.

My conditioned behavior versus glimpses of the absolute oneness of all.

So long as I have an inflexible opinion or preference, I will remain on
the teeter-totter of life–forever pushing and bouncing, up and down.
Unsure of who's sitting on the other end even though I know it's only me.

I never did like the teeter-totter.

LIBBY NICHOLSON

I've watched my mother turn from a self-absorbed bigot into a courageous soldier willing to take on her inner battle and fight for the treasures of self-discovery that were rightfully hers in the first place. A perfect model of "coming into existence." An example of fearlessness that makes me feel proud and safe.

Was she always that beautiful? I don't recall her being like that when I was young. Am I just noticing it now because I'm beginning to see the possibilities of my own depth?

It seems that as I heal, so does everybody else . . .

Why is it every time my heart gets broken I blame it on someone else?

Aren't I the one who gave it away ? Would it be safe to say that I'm the one who stuck it out there in the first place and allowed it to be chipped away?

Or am I still not ready to accept the responsibility for my own life?

Donald McIlraith

Dianne's grandmother used to send her fancy boxed stationery.
The kind with flowers and butterflies or kittens and ribbons.
She used to get so mad. She wanted a card with money tucked
inside instead.

As a kid I always coveted that pretty paper of hers. Yesterday I
asked her what ever happened to it all and she told me that she
used it to write letters to her grandmother after she died. They
contain all the things she wanted to say to her when she was alive
and didn't. She says they remind her to speak her heart now,
instead of later. They're all tied with a ribbon in a special place
where she can see them all the time.

I don't like what George said today. I'm so angry, I'm going to take my iron skillet out to the backyard and smash a circle of grass to dust and pretend it's his face.

If he's not going to do what I want him to do, at least I'll have the satisfaction of doing what *I* want to do.

Donald McIlraith

A woman I hardly knew told me I should cut my hair short. She also gave me advice to help make my appearance more agreeable to other people. When I sat down and considered her suggestions I had to laugh, because if she had her way she'd:

1) Pull out my two front teeth
2) Shave my head
3) Dress me in her wardrobe
4) Stretch me three inches taller

She judged me so condescendingly that I can only surmise that she must not feel very good about herself. I know from experience that the only time I'm dissatisfied with my appearance is when my inner self is out of sync. And nothing I do to the outside seems to right the internal disarray.

Donald McIlraith

CHRIS BLISS

I turned around today, took a long look at the past two years and realized that my old identity of "victim" seemed to have faded. Like waking up after a bad dream.

When did I start being responsible for my life? When did I realize that the results of my experiences were a direct reflection of my feelings–and my fears of my feelings? Somewhere along the line I must have realized that being a victim didn't work, rolled up my sleeves, and just started walking toward myself.

I don't remember when I started walking. I only remember noticing the good things about my day and, eventually, that was just about all I could see in everything. The good things.

Remember finger painting? Dipping your fingers into
the yellow and smearing them all over the paper?
Then the blue? The red?

Wow.

What great moments. Seeing that one thing mixed with
another does not equal one thing, but many things.

Add one more color and the whole spectrum changes,
and the possibilities multiply exponentially.

Add one more color . . . it boggles the mind.
The possibilities are endless.

Why did everyone stop finger-painting?

If man must conquer, then why doesn't he start with that great unknown territory—

himself.

Paul Hughes

Loving is like flying without a net. I let myself be vulnerable
and savor the moments. But when I encounter duplicity
instead of intimacy, the bond of trust is forever broken.
Then I cage my heart as an act of survival with intentions
of never letting it fly again. As time passes my courage
grows stronger, and I don't care how close to the bone
my wings have been clipped.

And what have I learned? I've learned how to love and
live a little bit more.

I accept that it's my nature to fly.

LIBBY J. NICHOLSON

I'm ready for the Rapture. The opening of the heavens.
The great awakening.

In the meantime, while I'm waiting, I'm going to enjoy
Ricky's chicken casserole surprise.

Nobody gets under my skin until I get there first.

CHRIS BLISS

CHRIS BLISS

Egotism. I've finally figured it out. It's just a basic survival instinct.
When someone appears to be overly boastful or conceited, it simply
means that they are insecure and feel it necessary to ring their bell
loudly, so as not to appear vulnerable. Because survival has always
depended on some kind of control.

Entire societies seem to follow this pattern. Entire countries want to
control other countries so as not to appear weak, then seek acceptance
and approval from the public for their actions. A basic survival
instinct driven by fear.

Do you think that if each one of us confronted our own personal
terror of vulnerability something wonderful might sweep the planet?
That personal freedom might trickle down the chain of command
from the commander-in-chief to the newspaper boy? Can anyone
envision a planet full of laughter?

N O T E
NUMBER
79

Here's a great corollary:

When I like myself

I GET EVERYTHING I WANT!

MARIANNE K. MCDONNELL

I am constantly at choice.

When I look out at the ocean, I can choose to see the horizon, the southward swells, seabirds riding the wind, white water and waves . . .

. . . or I can focus on the truth and see what's really there

. . . like the back of my head.

About twelve years ago a friend taught me how to put my arms around myself.
I felt stupid and awkward, sitting there in the dark, with my arms wrapped
around me, tight. I was surprised at myself when I started to cry. I cried
for a very long time.

When comfort finally came I felt like I had let go of a million lifetimes of pain.

A million lifetimes of seeking something outside of myself to show me the way.

A million lifetimes of hiding from the only one who could make a difference.

WARREN SAMUEL

NOTE
NUMBER
82

I used to wish that my Uncle Bob was my father. He has morals and values that are supportive, nurturing, and strong. Growing up under his large wings could have provided me with the love and guidance a kid needs.

Now I'm glad for all the pain and cruelties my own father subjected me to. The experiences made me strong and I cultivate myself from them. I can discern between lies and sincerity. I can love with tolerance.

I can face the pain, no longer afraid.

Patricia L. Goss

My heart is like a cool lake in the midst of summer
that I go skinny-dipping in every day.